Benjamin Scott

Lays of the Pilgrim Fathers

Benjamin Scott

Lays of the Pilgrim Fathers

ISBN/EAN: 9783337286897

Printed in Europe, USA, Canada, Australia, Japan

Cover: Foto ©Andreas Hilbeck / pixelio.de

More available books at **www.hansebooks.com**

Design, Memorial Church of the Pilgrim Fathers.

LAYS

OF THE

PILGRIM FATHERS;

COMPILED

IN AID OF THE FUND FOR COMPLETING

THE

𝕸emorial 𝕮hurch of the 𝕻ilgrim 𝕱athers,

IN SOUTHWARK.

BY

BENJAMIN SCOTT, F.R.A.S.,

CHAMBERLAIN OF LONDON, AND HON. SECRETARY OF THE WORKING MEN'S
EDUCATIONAL UNION.

> " From seeds they sowed with weeping,
>   Our richest harvests rise;
> We still the fruits are reaping
>   Of Pilgrim enterprise.
> Then gratefully to them we'll pay
>   The debt of fame we owe,
> Who planted freedom's sacred tree
>   Two hundred years ago."

LONDON:
LONGMAN, GREEN, LONGMAN, AND ROBERTS,
PATERNOSTER ROW.
MDCCCLXI.

LONDON:

T. HARRILD, PRINTER, SHOE LANE,

FLEET STREET.

INTRODUCTORY STATEMENT;

This is especially the age of memorials. A memorial, however, is a vain thing viewed merely as an expedient for preserving the memory of those of whom it is written, "the name of the wicked shall rot," and "their memorial is perished with them;" neither does it possess much value in relation to those benefactors of mankind whose deeds will necessarily be "had in everlasting remembrance" when the jealousies of contemporaries, and the passions and prejudices of party, shall have passed away; but, as the exponent of vital principles, or of truths discovered, vindicated, or rescued from neglect and oblivion, a memorial may be of service in fixing such principles and truths in men's minds, preserving definite impressions which the carelessness of mankind might otherwise efface.

We have, in many places, Scripture sanction for such memorials. Joshua, for instance, taking possession of the civil and religious privileges secured by territorial occupation of Canaan, set up "stones of memorial unto the children of Israel for ever:" and "he spake unto the children of Israel, saying, 'When your children shall ask their fathers in time to come, saying, What mean these stones? then ye shall let your children know, saying. . . . That *all the people of the earth* might know the hand of the Lord, that it is mighty; and that *ye* might fear the Lord your God for ever."—(Josh. iv.)

It had occurred, some ten years since, to earnest and thoughtful men, that, notwithstanding the light and liberty at present enjoyed, many advantages would attend the erection of a memorial which should remind the present, and keep informed the coming generations, of the martyrdom, sufferings, and privations of those who were the fathers of restored freedom of conscience and free worship in the *old* world, and who became the founders of an empire of free worshippers in the *new*. It was felicitously suggested that a memorial building, comprising Lecture-hall, Church, and School-rooms, should be erected, as nearly as circumstances would permit, on the site of the place of meeting of the first *Separatists* of Southwark (the precursors, from 1559 to 1620, of the expatriated Pilgrim Fathers of New England), in the vicinity of the prisons* in which so many of their members were immured, and near to

* The Clink and the King's Bench.

the spot where their pastor, PENRY, was, for maintaining their principles, brought to a martyr's grave. *

The attention of the friends of religious freedom was directed to the suggested memorial by the Rev. Thomas Binney, in a paper drawn up and subscribed by himself, and subsequently subscribed by the leading ministers of the Congregational body. As it is impossible to improve upon this statement, it is transcribed in this place, to speak for itself on behalf of the Pilgrims' Memorial :—

"MEMORIAL CHURCH OF THE PILGRIM FATHERS, SOUTHWARK.

"The Church and Congregation assembling in UNION STREET CHAPEL, SOUTHWARK, being under the necessity of soon quitting it, propose to erect, in some conspicuous situation in the neighbourhood, a new place of worship under the above title.

"Southwark is famous in the annals of Nonconformity, and was intimately connected, in various ways, with those eminent and heroic men who laid the foundations of society in New England. During the latter half of the sixteenth century, some of the most distinguished Puritan (Separatist†) confessors and martyrs found in Southwark a home, a church, a prison, and a grave.

"In 1586, JOHN GREENWOOD was a prisoner in the *Clink*, a place of confinement close to St. Saviour's Church, for advocating, in ecclesiastical arrangements, what he regarded as an approach to the purity and order of Apostolic times.

"HENRY BARROWE, another defender of the same views, calling upon GREENWOOD on a Sunday morning, under the impulse of Christian sympathy, 'remembering them that were in bonds as

* St. Thomas-a-Watering, Old Kent Road ; about half a mile from the selected site of the Memorial Church.

† See foot-note at page 50.

bound with them,' was literally secured and detained by the jailer, carried to Lambeth, and presented as a prisoner to the Archbishop.

"In 1593, these men, in the hope of their constancy being shaken, were twice taken from the prison to the gibbet, and reprieved at the last moment. The first time they were led to the foot of the gallows; the second time the ropes were about their necks, and they stood some minutes in the expectation of immediate death, before the reprieve was produced. Nothing could affect them. In a few days they were hanged!

"In the same month John Penry was taken from his cell in the King's Bench prison, Southwark, and executed at St. Thomas-a-Watering, Old Kent Road, for Nonconformity!

"Francis Johnson, while a prisoner in the *Clink* for the same '*crime*,' wrote, in 1596, a defence of Separation, which converted an antagonist, who had forwarded 'an argument' to convert *him*. This convert was Henry Jacob, who, as a man of learning, piety, and zeal, soon became celebrated among the Separatists.

"Henry Jacob resided for some time on the Continent, where he came into contact with Robinson, from whose church went the emigrants who sailed in the *Mayflower*, landed at Plymouth Rock, and became known in history as ' The Pilgrim Fathers.'

"In 1616,* the first Independent Church in England was formed IN Southwark, by this Henry Jacob, and some twenty or thirty others who united with him. 'They observed a day of solemn fasting and prayer; made, severally, a confession of their faith in Christ; and then, standing up together, they joined hands, and solemnly covenanted with each other, in the presence of Almighty God, to walk together in all God's ways and ordinances, according as He had already revealed, or should further make them known to them.'

"Mr. Jacob was chosen and constituted the pastor of this Church; but, after a service of eight years, crossed the Atlantic to join 'the Pilgrims' in America. He, however, reached their resting-place only *to die*. His career closed soon after he touched the shore; he

* Since the above was penned, in 1853, the track of the hidden Separatist Church has been traced back to the year 1559. See work by Dr. Waddington, alluded to in foot-note, page 17.

was not allowed to fulfil his purpose in joining his friends, but he found in the midst of them an appropriate grave.

"JOHN LATHROP succeeded Mr. JACOB as pastor of the Church in Southwark. In 1632, he and some forty of the members of his Church were apprehended and sentenced to imprisonment for two years! While undergoing this punishment, Mr. Lathrop procured permission from the bishop to visit his wife on her dying bed. He went,—commended her soul to God,—and *returned to jail*. He had a large family ; his children, deprived of both parents, petitioned for their father's liberty ; the remainder of his sentence was remitted ; and, towards the close of 1634, he, with thirty of his Church, joined ' the Pilgrims' in New England.

In 1641, the Church being assembled on Lord's-day for worship, but with less than usual secrecy, they were discovered and taken to the *Clink*. Six or seven of the members appeared before the House of Lords, and received a reprimand. They were ordered ' to repair to the parish church to hear Divine service according to the Acts of Parliament.' They repaired to their own place, and, on the next Sunday, conducted Divine service according to their convictions of the mind and will of God. Three or four peers, interested by what they heard and saw when the men were before them, actually attended and witnessed their proceedings, hearing two sermons on the words, ' All power is given unto ME in heaven and in earth.' They thus heard, no doubt, of ONE whose power was superior to that of any secular assembly, how dignified soever ; and they would see, too, the calm confidence of men, who, in the midst of persecution, relying on that power, could exult and sing—

      " ' God is our refuge, tried and proved
        Amid a stormy world ;
      We will not fear, though earth be moved
        And hills in ocean hurl'd.
      When earth and hell against us came,
        He spake, and quell'd their powers :
      The Lord of Hosts is still the same—
        The God of Grace is ours.'

"It is unnecessary to add to the above deeply interesting and suggestive facts. It was thus that SOUTHWARK was hallowed and sanctified in past times, by its being the birth-place of the first British Congregational church; by the confessors and martyrs of Puritanism and Nonconformity being pursued within it to prison and to death; by its little Church receiving its first pastor from under the influence of ROBINSON,—the founder of Independency, as purified from the excesses of Brownism, and inspired with a catholic spirit,—the *father* of those who became the *Pilgrim* Fathers; and by many from itself joining the Pilgrims in their distant home.

"Of the constant, persecuted, and prolific *Nonconformity* of Southwark, the Union Street Church is the principal representative. The intention of this Church to erect what shall be at once a suitable home for itself, and a fitting MONUMENT to its noble ancestry, commends itself alike to the judgment and the heart. It must obtain sympathy and approval on all hands. It is adapted to excite interest on both sides of the Atlantic—*it should attract aid from every part of the kingdom.* Let the work be done, and done well. Let ministers and deacons—the members of our many churches and congregations—all, to whom Truth and Liberty are dear—let them patronize the object, and put a brick in the building.

"In these days of revived ritualism, of excessive ecclesiastical pretensions and claims, of Popish inroads and Popish conversions, let there be in this great metropolis *one* structure, commanding and conspicuous, that shall commemorate the advocates of a simple polity and a Scriptural creed, and that may turn the attention of observers to the study of their history—a history more pregnant with instruction for *these our times* than any other in the world.

"THOMAS BINNEY.

"*London, January,* 1853.

"We, the undersigned, unite to commend the object of our friends in Southwark to all with whom we may have influence, willingly pledging ourselves by this act to aid them, by word or deed, to the utmost of our power.

James Bennett, D.D.	John Leifchild, D.D.	John Harris, D.D.
John Campbell, D.D.	J. W. Massie, D.D.,	W. H. Stowell, D.D.
Henry Allon.	LL.D.	Jos. Turnbull, B.A.

James Carlile, D.D.	J. E. Richards.	Thomas Timpson.
E. Henderson, D.D.	J. De Kewer Williams.	Thomas Muscutt.
Philip Smith, B.A.	George Thomson.	Robert Ainslie.
George Smith.	Thomas James.	John Robinson.
Richard Fletcher, Manchester.	Henry Richard.	John Chapman Davie.
	David Thomas.	G. R. Birch.
John Hoppus, LL.D., F.R.S.	George Rogers.	Charles Gilbert.
	Evan Davies.	T. Davies.
Samuel Ransom, M.A.	William Tyler.	W. Spencer Edwards.
John Morison, D.D., LL.D.	B. S. Hollis.	D. Davies.
	George Wilkins.	H. Seaborn.
William Campbell, M.A.	Samuel Roberts.	John Davies.
	William Rees.	W. Owen.
William Bean.	William Owen.	S. S. England.
Ralph Wardlaw, D.D.	J. C. Harrison.	Robert Ashton.
J. C. Gallaway, M.A.	J. W. Richardson.	Benjamin Kent.
James Sherman.	J. Baldwin Brown, B.A.	Ebenezer Davies.
John Stoughton.		John Kennedy, M.A.
John Hunt.	Charles Fox Vardy, M.A.	W. P. Davies.
James Hill.		A. Good.
John Adey.	Robert Littler.	John Hall.
William Leask.	Robert Philip.	William Forster.
Josiah Viney.	John Bramall.	Charles Williams."
George Rose.	J. P. Dobson.	

The CONGREGATIONAL UNION of England and Wales considered the subject of sufficient importance to engage their consideration. At a meeting held in the year 1855, a motion, proposed by the late Rev. Dr. Harris, seconded by the Rev. J. Stoughton, and supported by several leading members of that body, was unanimously adopted, expressive of " deep interest in the project," and commending it " to the prompt and generous sympathy and support of the Christian public." (" Congregational Year Book," 1856, p. 67.)

The intimate connection between the persecuted Separatists of Southwark and the founders of the first

North American settlement, could not fail to interest
the United States Ambassador to this country with
respect to the proposed memorial. The Honourable
Abbott Lawrence accordingly addressed to Mr. Waddington, the pastor of the Church in Southwark, a
letter which manifests the deep interest which was
taken in the proposal by that lamented statesman.

"In common," says he, "with most of my countrymen, I enter-
tain the most profound and sincere reverence for the memory of
the band of heroic Christians, who, in the face, in the Old World,
of neglect and oppression; and, in the New, of terrific trials, of
countless dangers, of death from cold, from starvation, and from a
treacherous foe, founded a Christian colony, which has now grown
into one of the great nations of the earth. If that nation has proved
to the world that religious freedom and religious faith may flourish
together, or that perfect liberty and perfect law are not incompatible,
I attribute it, in no slight degree, to the deep and permanent influence which the principles of Brewster and Robinson, Carver and
Bradford, and their little commonwealth, have had upon its cha-
racter.

"It seems superfluous to speak of this little community of men
and women (NOBLE WOMEN, too), which has now become one of the
admirations of the world, and which gathered within its ranks as
great, I believe, if not greater, an amount of Christian faith, forti-
tude, endurance, and hope, than was ever found in a body of equal
numbers on earth. The 'Rock of Plymouth,' where they finally
made their home, has become our Mecca, to which we annually, on
the wintry anniversary of their landing, make a pilgrimage, to renew
our vows of fidelity to the principles of our forefathers, and offer up
our thankful devotions to their and our God for the civil and religious liberty He has permitted us to inherit from them. Long may
that rock remain—a monument to teach my countrymen so to con-
duct the affairs of the present, that the future may not be unworthy
of the past we have received.

" The influence of their example is not confined to the land where it was displayed. *Europe has begun to study their principles;* and I think I see their influence increasing in this country. I am proud when I see efforts like the present to extend among the British people a just knowledge of these English men and women. You, too, may well be proud to be the pastor of a Church where they preached and worshipped, and may appeal without fear to our brethren, both in England and throughout the world, to come forward and erect a church in commemoration of an event, the effects of which, already deeply felt, are destined probably to influence the world more than any other in modern history."

Mr. Lawrence is not the only warm friend to the cause whom death has removed. The late respected and lamented Lord Mayor of London (Mr. Alderman Wire), to the time of his death, took a deep interest in the Memorial Church, and was most solicitous that it should be speedily completed.

The LONDON CHAPEL BUILDING SOCIETY, constrained by their constitution and duties to take a merely local and strictly religious view of the proposal, have resolved to countenance the project so far as it contemplates provision for the ministrations of religion in a district containing a vast population very destitute of spiritual advantages, and have voted a liberal grant in aid.

So much for the sanctions under which the suggestion has been inaugurated; sufficient, in my judgment, to warrant my treatment of it as a denominational object with the Congregational body, and to encourage me to anticipate their almost unanimous suffrages when I appeal to them to put a speedy finish to a work so worthy of their support.

It may be necessary to state, for the information of some, that delay and disappointment, ' with consequent increase of outlay, have arisen from personal divergence of opinion and divided counsels on the part of those who, in time past, were engaged in giving direction to the undertaking. Had this not been so, it is reasonable to conclude that the matter would ere this have approached completion. Profitless is it to reopen a discussion now happily at rest, and vain the endeavour to arrive at a satisfactory conclusion as to the causes of disagreement. The object is, fortunately, not of personal, but of national—nay, of universal—interest. The principles involved rise superior to all minor considerations. They should neither be postponed nor set aside by merely personal and temporary hindrances, or by the infirmities of human agency: their issues are world-wide and everlasting.

To a rightly-constituted mind it will be refreshing to turn from personal considerations to principles. In this spirit, breathed in the admirable documents penned by Mr. Lawrence and Mr. Binney, let us set about redeeming the pledge given by the Congregational body. Those who have most regretted the interruption of the work will feel the liveliest interest (for the sake of the moral influence of the case) in raising the unfinished walls. Providence has given us the opportunity. Impressed with the desirableness of seizing it with promptitude, I have felt that it would be a work in accordance with the best feelings of my Congregational brethren (Independent and Baptist) to bring the subject once more before their notice.

What, then, are the facts of the case as it now stands? The Memorial Hall, erected in Buckenham Square, is complete, and is used for the purposes of the church there assembling; while the School-room beneath is occupied by an interesting Sabbath-school, numbering some one hundred and sixty children. Both buildings are occupied to the extent of accommodation afforded. The church members are gradually increasing in number, and there exists a cheering spirit of unanimity. The feeling of interest in the neighbourhood is also encouraging, as the writer of these lines can testify. The undertaking stands now quite free from debt, liability, complication, or embarrassment. All outstanding accounts have been paid, the building covenants on which the ground is held have been satisfied, and the foundations of the whole structure are put in.

The sole remaining difficulty—if such it can be termed—is a *pecuniary* one. This might be removed in a week, if the Congregational body were alive to the importance of the object and the dignity of their position

with reference thereto.   The elegant design which has
been partially erected (*vide* frontispiece) should, without further delay, be completed.   To use Mr. Binney's
words, "let the work be done, and done well.   Let
ministers and deacons, the members of our many
churches and congregations, all to whom Truth and
Liberty are dear, let them patronize the object, and put
a brick in the building."   The occasion is not one for
the exercise of a niggard economy, and honour to those
who have already contributed forbids that any material
deviation in plan be entertained.   The erection, which
in future ages will be visited by the descendants of the
Pilgrims from across the Atlantic, should be worthy of
those whom it commemorates, and of the twin countries
in connection with which it will stand as a connecting-
link.   *Our Transatlantic brethren are expending £40,000
on the erection of the "Plymouth Memorial."   Shall it be
said that we cannot raise, or care not to raise, less than a
tithe of that sum to complete a memorial dedicated to the
same sacred and eternal principles?*

It is estimated that some £3500 will complete the
memorial building.   The sums already promised by a
few friends in London, and the grant voted by the London Chapel Building Society will provide about £500.
Say, then, that £3000 is the amount now required of
the great Congregational body in England and Wales as
a thank-offering for the inestimable privilege of " FREE-

DOM TO WORSHIP GOD," obtained for them by the patient and persistent endurance, even unto death, of the confessors and martyrs whose names and principles it is proposed to hand down to an admiring posterity.

This sum will not amount, on an average, to fifty shillings per church, and many of them would be ashamed to contribute so small a sum as five times that amount. *Shall the thing be done, and the reproach of indifference be swept away?* Shall it result from this and former humble efforts to throw light upon and excite interest in this subject* that, by a general co-operation, the projected memorial be removed from the category in which it now stands ? reminding us unpleasantly of the illustration of our Lord : " Which of you, intending to build a tower, sitteth not down first, and counteth the cost, whether ye have sufficient to finish it ? Lest haply, after he hath laid the foundation, and is not able to finish it, all that behold it begin to mock him, saying, This man began to build, and was not able to finish."†

But, in place of arousing the *amour propre* of the denomination, I prefer greatly to appeal to those grateful feelings, which a little reflection on their past history

* A set of twelve large pictures or diagrams on the Pilgrim Fathers has been recently published, and the compiler has also published a lecture to accompany them (*vide* advertisement at end). Dr. Waddington has likewise, at the solicitation of American friends, prepared a volume for distribution through their churches, entitled "The Track of the Hidden Church ; or, the Springs of the Pilgrim Movement, from A.D. 1559 to 1620." This work is ready in America, and will shortly be attainable in London.

† Luke xiv. 28—30.

will not fail to excite—feelings which have furnished in-
spiration to the Poets whose "lays" I have selected for
publication in the following pages.

> "Oh! many a time it hath been told,
> The story of those men of old :
> For *them* fair Poetry hath wreathed
>   Her sweetest, fairest flower ;
> For *them* proud Eloquence hath breathed
>   His strain of loftiest power.
>
> Twine, GRATITUDE, a wreath for them,
> More deathless than the diadem ;
> Who, to life's noblest end,
>   Gave up life's noblest powers,
> AND BADE THE LEGACY DESCEND
>   DOWN, DOWN TO US AND OURS."

The following Gentlemen have consented to act as Trustees and
    joint Treasurers of Funds contributed for the Completion of
    the Memorial. These funds will be held in reserve until the
    structure can be finished in accordance with the original
    design, and to the satisfaction of the London Chapel Building
    Society :—

WILLIAM ARMITAGE, Esq., Manchester.   } *Surviving*
APSLEY PELLATT, Esq., Southwark.   } *Trustees.*
SAMUEL MORLEY, Esq., London.   } *New*
BENJAMIN SCOTT, Esq., Chamberlain, London. } *Trustees.*

CONTENTS.

LAYS OF THE PILGRIM FATHERS.

THE PILGRIMS' FAREWELL TO ENGLAND.

THE breeze has swelled the whitening sail,
The blue waves curl beneath the gale,
And, bounding with the wave and wind,
We leave Old England's shores behind—
 Leave behind our native shore,
 Homes, and all we loved before.

The deep may dash, the winds may blow,
The storm spread out its wings of woe,
Till sailors' eyes can see a shroud
Hung in the folds of every cloud :
 Still, as long as life shall last,
 From that shore we'll speed us fast.

For we would rather never be,
Than dwell where mind cannot be free,
But bows beneath a despot's rod,
E'en where it seeks to worship God.
    Blasts of heaven, onward sweep!
    Bear us o'er the troubled deep!

O, see what wonders meet our eyes!
Another land, and other skies!
Columbia's hills have met our view!
Adieu! Old England's shores, adieu!
    Here, at length, our feet shall rest,
    Hearts be free, and homes be blessed.

As long as yonder firs shall spread
Their green arms o'er the mountain's head—
As long as yonder cliffs shall stand,
Where join the ocean and the land,—
    Shall those cliffs and mountains be
    Proud retreats for liberty.

                              T. C. UPHAM.

THE PILGRIMS AT ANCHOR.

THE breaking waves dashed high,
   On a stern and rock-bound coast;
And the woods, against a stormy sky,
   Their giant branches tost;
And the heavy night hung dark,
   The hills and waters o'er,
When a band of exiles moored their bark
   On the wild New England shore.

Not as the conqueror comes,
   They, the true-hearted, came;
Not with the stirring roll of drums,
   And the trumpet that sings of fame.
Not as the flying come,
   In silence and in fear—
They shook the depths of the desert gloom
   With their hymns of lofty cheer.

Amid the storm they sang,
　And the stars heard, and the sea;
And the sounding aisles of the dim woods rang
　With the anthem of the free!
The ocean eagle soared
　From his nest by the white waves' foam,
And the rocking pines of the forest roared;
　This was their welcome home.

There were men with hoary hair
　Amid that pilgrim band;
Why had they come to wither there,
　Away from their childhood's land?
There was woman's fearless eye,
　Lit by her deep love's truth;
There was manhood's brow serenely high,
　And the fiery heart of youth.

What sought they thus afar?
　Bright jewels of the mine?
The wealth of seas? the spoils of war?—
　They sought a faith's pure shrine!
Ay, call it holy ground,
　The soil where first they trod:
They have left unstained what there they found—
　FREEDOM TO WORSHIP GOD!

FELICIA HEMANS.

At a Pilgrim celebration in Boston, held November 11th, 1851, the Rev. Charles Brooks said:—"It may not be uninteresting to state the cause and occasion of the writing of that popular little poem on the 'Landing of Pilgrim Fathers,' by Mrs. Hemans. During a short and delightful stay at her house in Dublin, Ireland, in July, 1834, I had a long conversation with her. She expressed a deep interest in the United States; and said that she had been better understood in Massachusetts than in England.

"I told her that, as a member of the Old Colony Pilgrim Society, I had a right to thank her, in their name, for her true and touching little poem on the landing of the Pilgrim Fathers. 'Well,' said she, 'should you like to know how I came to write it? I purchased two volumes at the bookstore, and brought them home, and, as I laid them on my table, my eye was attracted by their envelope, which proved to be eight pages 8vo of an address delivered at Plymouth on some anniversary. The excellence of the paper and the beauty of the type arrested my attention; but how this stray fragment got to Ireland, I could never ascertain. I began to read, and I found it contained an entire description of the fact of landing, and so beautiful was the painting, and so thrilling the fact, that I could not rest till I had thrown them into verse. I took off my bonnet, seized my pen, and, having read and re-read the story, I caught the fire from this transatlantic torch, and began to write, and before I was aware I had finished my poem.'

" I then told her how much we valued the lines for their truthfulness and spirit, and how I had stood with a thousand persons in the old Pilgrim Church, at Plymouth, on 'Forefathers' Day,' and sung with them her exquisite hymn. At this remark a tear stole into her eye. 'But,' said I, 'my dear madam, there are two lines of that poem which the descendants of the pilgrims prize above the rest.' 'Ah! which are they?' I began to repeat—'They left unstained what there they found;' 'O! yes,' said she, interrupting me hastily, and then reciting the next line, 'Freedom to worship God.' 'Yes,' I replied, 'Freedom to worship God.' Then raising her voice, her eye at the same moment beaming with religious enthusiasm, she exclaimed: 'It is the TRUTH there, which makes the poetry.'

" When about to say farewell to this charming lady, she took my hand, and said—'When you next meet with your Pilgrim Society, present them my heart-felt thanks for their flattering partiality towards me, and tell them that I wish every one of them prosperity and happiness.' "

HYMN.

God of our fathers, to Thy throne
    Our grateful songs we raise ;
Thou art our God, and Thou alone,—
    Accept our humble praise.

Unnumbered benefits from Thee
    Are showered upon our land ;
Behold ! through all our coasts we see
    The bounties of Thy hand.

Here Thou wert once the Pilgrims' guide ;
    Thou gav'st them here a place,
Where freedom spreads its blessings wide,
    O'er all their favoured race.

Here, Lord, Thy gospel's holy light
    Is shed on all our hills ;
And, like the rains and dews of night,
    Celestial grace distils.

Still teach us, Lord, Thy name to fear,
    And still our guardian be ;
O let our children's children here
    For ever worship Thee.

THE MAYFLOWER.

O, little Fleet!—that, on thy quest divine,
 Sailedst from Palos one bright autumn morn,—
 Say, has Old Ocean's bosom ever borne
A freight of Faith and Hope, to match with thine?

Say, too, has Heaven's high favour given again
 Such consummation of desire, as shone
 About Columbus, when he rested on
The new-found world and married it to Spain?

Answer, thou refuge of the freeman's need,
 Thou for whose destinies no kings looked out,
 Nor sages to resolve some mighty doubt,
Thou simple Mayflower of the salt-sea mead!

When *thou* wert wafted to that distant shore,
 Gay flowers, bright birds, rich odours, met thee not,
 Stern nature hail'd thee to a sterner lot—
God gave free earth and air, and gave no more.

Thus to men cast in that heroic mould
 Came empire, such as Spaniard never knew—
 Such empire as beseems the just and true;
And at the last, almost unsought, came gold.

But He, who rules both calm and stormy days,
 Can guard that people's heart, that nation's health,
 Safe on the perilous heights of power and wealth,
As in the straitness of the ancient ways.

RICHARD MONCKTON MILNES.

CLARK'S ISLAND.*

HAIL, hallowed spot ! where Freedom's rays
First darted o'er the wanderer's ways,
    And gave him rest ;
First brought the dawn of brighter days,
    Thy shores are blest !
But dark the clouds that lingered round
The island which the Pilgrims found,
    In time long gone ;
And deep and drear the thrilling sound
    Of gathering storm.

Aye, dark indeed, the night of yore,
That rocked the Mayflower near thy shore
    On wintry tides ;
For dark the waves that round thee roar,
    And wash thy sides.

* A small island at the entrance of Plymouth Bay, Mass. At the highest
point of land is a gray rock, commanding a view of the surrounding shores.
Here the Pilgrims, having posted a sentinel, kept their first Sabbath in New
England. Under the shelter of this gray rock the pastor of the Church of the
Pilgrim Fathers in Southwark united in worship with descendants of the
Pilgrims. On the day when the foundation-stone of the Monument at Ply-
mouth was laid, Dr. Waddington also stood on the rock where the Pilgrims
landed after leaving Clark's Island, and offered prayer for America and England.

But bright the star that lent its ray
To bear the traveller on his way
      From childhood's seat,
That lighted up so fair a day
      For his retreat.

Oh, who would ask a holier bed
Than where he laid his weary head
      And nobly slept;
For though the Pilgrim long hath fled,
      His spirit's left.
Then hail the spot, where first the sound
Of freedom shook the sacred ground
      In early days,
And filled the hills and forest round
      With gladsome praise.

HERSEY B. GOODWIN.

LANDING OF THE PILGRIMS.

WILD was the day; the wintry sea
   Moaned sadly on New England's strand
When first, the thoughtful and the free,
   Our fathers trod the desert land.

They little thought how pure a light,
   With years, should gather round that day;
How love should keep their memories bright,
   How wide a realm their sons should sway.

Green are their bays, and greener still
   Shall round their spreading fame be wreathed;
And regions now untrod shall thrill
   With reverence when their names are breathed.

Till where the sun, with softer fires,
   Looks on the vast Pacific's sleep,
The children of the Pilgrim sires
   This hallowed day like us shall keep.*

W. C. BRYANT.

* "FOREFATHERS' DAY," December the 22nd, the anniversary of the landing
at the Plymouth Rock.

THE PILGRIMS' FIRST SABBATH.

THE modest Isle of yonder Bay,*
Screened from the rougher blasts and spray,
There, long by storm and billow driven,
With mast and sail to fragments riven,
The wanderers sought its welcome shore,
And safe their struggling shallop moor;
There watchful met the earliest dawn,
When first revealed the Sabbath morn,
That prayer and praise might o'er the deep
Harmonious strains in concert keep.

New England's pristine Sabbath-day
On Time's dark flood has passed away;
The Pilgrim chant is heard no more,
That echoed once upon that shore;
And hushed the lips whose accents gave
Their grateful notes to wind and wave;
But still the Sabbath's cheerful hours
Shall claim and bless our noblest powers,
And wing our thoughts to scenes divine,
Where faith and hope no more decline.

* Clark's Island. Then came the Sabbath; they had been three days from
their friends; the Captain was in haste to be gone, but nothing would induce
them to move. A sentinel was posted, and the party, under the shelter of a
gray rock, kept the first Christian Sabbath in New England.

PILGRIMS AT PRAYER.

THE winds and waves were roaring,
　　The Pilgrims met for prayer ;
And here, their God adoring,
　　They stood in open air :
When breaking day they greeted,
　　And when its close was calm,
The leafless woods repeated
　　The music of their psalm.

Not thus, O God, to praise Thee
　　Do we, their children, throng ;
The temple's arch we raise Thee
　　Gives back our choral song.
Yet, on the winds that bore Thee
　　Their worship and their prayers,
May ours come up before Thee
　　From hearts as true as theirs !

What have we, Lord, to bind us
　　To this, the Pilgrims' shore ?
Their hill of graves behind us,
　　Their watery way before ;

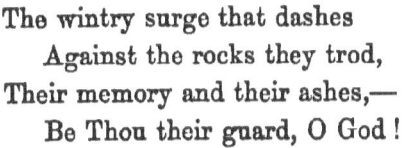

The wintry surge that dashes
    Against the rocks they trod,
Their memory and their ashes,—
    Be Thou their guard, O God !

We would not, Holy Father,
    Forsake this hallow'd spot,
Till on that shore we gather
    Where graves and griefs are not,—
The shore where true devotion
    Shall rear no pillar'd shrine,
And see no other ocean
    Than that of love divine.

REV. JOHN PIERPOINT.

HOME OF THE PILGRIMS.

Over the mountain wave, see where they come !
Storm-cloud and wintry wind welcome them home ;
Yet, where the sounding gale howls to the sea,
There their song peals along, deep-toned and free :
    " Pilgrims and wanderers, hither we come,
    Where the free dare to be—this is our home !"

England hath sunny dales, dearly they bloom ;
Scotia hath heather bells, sweet their perfume ;
Yet through the wilderness cheerful we stray,
Native land, native land—home far away !
    " Pilgrims and wanderers, hither we come,
    Where the free dare to be—this is our home !"

Dim grew the forest-path ; onward they trod ;
Firm beat their noble hearts, trusting in God.
Gray men and blooming maids, high rose their song ;
Hear it sweep, clear and deep, ever along—
    " Pilgrims and wanderers, hither we come,
    Where the free dare to be—this is our home !"

Not theirs the glory wreath, torn by the blast ;
Heavenward their holy steps, heavenward they pass'd !
Green be their mossy graves, ours be their fame !
While their song peals along, ever the same—
    " Pilgrims and wanderers, hither we come,
    Where the free dare to be—this our home !"

GEORGE LUNT.

PILGRIMS IN SUNNY CLIMES.*

WHERE the remote Bermudas ride
In th' ocean's bosom unespy'd;
From a small boat that row'd along,
The list'ning wind received this song:—

" What should we do but sing His praise,
That led us through the wat'ry maze,
Unto an isle so long unknown,
And yet far kinder than our own?
Where He the huge sea-monster wracks,
That lift the deep upon their backs.
He lands us on a grassy stage,
Safe from the storms' and prelates' rage.
He gave us this eternal spring,
Which here enamels every thing;
And sends the fowls to us in care,
On daily visits through the air.

* The above lines do not refer to the Pilgrim Fathers, but to a settlement at
the Bermudas under somewhat similar circumstances, as is evidenced by the
allusion to immunity from persecution for conscience sake. By the third patent
of the Virginia Company, granted in 1612, the Bermudas, and all islands within
three hundred leagues of the coast, were included within the limits of their juris-
diction. These islands they sold to 120 of their own members, who became a dis-
tinct corporation, under the name of the Somers' Islands Company.—See "Stith's
Virginia," p. 127, App. 4.

George Mourt, writing of the Pilgrims of Plymouth, says:—"The
example of the Honourable Virginia and Bermudas Companies encountering
with so many disasters, and that for divers years together, with an unwearied
resolution, the good effects whereof are now eminent, may prevail as a spur of
preparation also, touching this no less hopeful country. Though yet an infant,
their extent and commodities are as yet not fully known; aftertime will unfold
more."

He hangs in shades the orange bright,
Like golden lamps in a green night;
And does in the pomegranates close
Jewels more rich than ocean shows.
He makes the figs our mouths to meet,
And throws the melons at our feet;
But apples plants of such a price,
No tree could ever bear them twice.
With cedars chosen by His hand,
From Lebanon, He stores the land;
And makes the hollow seas that roar
Proclaim the ambergrease on shore.
He cast (of which we rather boast)
The Gospel's pearl upon our coast;
And in these rocks for us did frame
A temple, where to sound His name.
Oh! let our voice His praise exalt,
Till it arrive at heaven's vault;
Which, then (perhaps) rebounding, may
Echo beyond the Mexique Bay."

Thus sung they, in the English boat,
An holy and a cheerful note;
And all the way, to guide their chime,
With falling oars they kept the time.

ANDREW MARVELL.

THE MISSION OF THE PILGRIMS.

THEY come—that coming who shall tell?
The eye may weep, the breast may swell;
But the poor tongue in vain essays
A fitting note for them to raise.
We hear the after-shout that rings
For them who smote the power of kings;
The swelling triumph all would share:
But who the dark defeat would dare,
And boldly meet the wrath and woe
That wait the unsuccessful blow?

It were an envied fate, we deem,
To live a land's recorded theme
　　When we are in the tomb.
We, too, might yield the joys of home,
And waves of winter darkness roam,
　　And tread a shore of gloom,
Knew we those waves, through coming time,
Should roll our names to every clime;
Felt we that millions on that shore
Should stand, our memory to adore.
But no glad vision burst in light
Upon the pilgrim's aching sight;

Their hearts no proud hereafter swelled ;
Deep shadows veiled the way they held ;
The yell of vengeance was the trump of fame ;
Their monument, a grave without a name.

Yet strong in weakness, there they stand
    On yonder icebound rock,
Stern and resolved, that faithful band,
    To meet fate's rudest shock.
Though anguish rends the father's breast,
For them, his dearest and his best,
    With him the waste who trod ;
Though tears that freeze the mother sheds
Upon her children's houseless heads—
    The Christian turns to God !

In grateful adoration now,
Upon the barren sands they bow ;
What tongue of joy e'er woke such prayer
As bursts in desolation there !
What arm of strength e'er wrought such power
As waits to crown that feeble hour !
    There into life an infant empire springs !
There falls the iron from the soul,
There Liberty's young accents roll
    Up to the King of kings !
To fair creation's farthest bound
That thrilling summons yet shall sound ;
The dreaming nations shall awake,
And to their centre earth's old kingdoms shake.

Pontiff and Prince, your sway
Must crumble from that day.
Before the loftier throne of Heaven,
The band is raised, the pledge is given—
One monarch to obey, one creed to own:
That monarch, God; that creed, His Word alone.

Spread out earth's holiest records here,
Of days and deeds to reverence dear.
A zeal like this what pious legends tell!
On kingdoms built
In blood and guilt,
The worshippers of vulgar triumph dwell.
But what exploits with theirs shall page
Who rose to bless their kind,
Who left their nation and their age,
Man's spirit to unbind?
Who boundless seas passed o'er
And boldly met, in every path,
Famine, and frost, and heathen wrath,
To dedicate a shore,
Where Piety's meek train might breathe their vow,
And seek their Maker with an unshamed brow;
Where Liberty's glad race might proudly come,
And set up there an everlasting home!

O, many a time it hath been told,
The story of those men of old:

For this fair Poetry hath wreathed
    Her sweetest, purest flower;
For this proud Eloquence hath breathed
    His strain of loftiest power:
Devotion, too, hath lingered round
Each spot of consecrated ground,
    And hill and valley blessed;
There, where our banished fathers strayed,
There, where they loved, and wept, and prayed,
    There, where their ashes rest.
And never may they rest unsung
While Liberty can find a tongue.
Twine, Gratitude, a wreath for them,
More deathless than the diadem,
Who, to life's noblest end,
    Gave up life's noblest powers,
And bade the legacy descend,
    Down, down to us and ours.

Sprague.

PILGRIMS' VOW.

How slow yon tiny vessel ploughs the main!
Amid the heavy billows now she seems
A toiling atom,—then from wave to wave
Leaps madly, by the tempest lashed,—or reels,
Half wrecked, through gulfs profound.
                 — Moons wax and wane,
But still that lonely traveller treads the deep.—
I see an icebound coast, toward which she steers
With such a tardy movement, that it seems
Stern Winter's hand hath turned her keel to stone,
And scaled his victory on her slippery shrouds.
They land!—they land!—not like the Genoese,
With glittering sword, and gaudy train, and eye
Kindling with golden fancies.   Forth they come
From their long prison—hardy forms, that brave
The world's unkindness—men of hoary hair,
And virgins of firm heart, and matrons grave,
Who hush the wailing infant with a glance.—
Bleak Nature's desolation wraps them round,
Eternal forests, or unyielding earth,
And savage men, who through the thickets peer
With vengeful arrow.—What could lure their steps
To this drear desert?—Ask of him who left
His father's house to roam through Haran's wilds,
Distrusting not the Guide who called him forth,

Nor doubting, though a stranger, that his seed
Should be as Ocean's sands. —
                    But yon lone bark
Hath spread her parting sail.

                    They crowd the strand,
Those few lone pilgrims.— Can ye scan the woe
That wrings their bosoms, as the last frail link,
Binding to man and habitable earth,
Is severed ?—Can ye tell what pangs were there,
What keen regrets, what sickness of the heart,
What yearnings o'er their forfeit land of birth,
Their distant dear ones ?

                    Long, with straining eye
They watch the lessening speck.   Heard ye no shriek
Of anguish, when that bitter loneliness
Sank down into their bosoms ?—No, they turn
Back to their dreary, famished huts, and pray !—
Pray,—and the ills that haunt this transient life
Fade into air.—Up in each girded breast
There sprang a rooted and mysterious strength—
A loftiness—to face a world in arms,—
To strip the pomp from sceptres,—and to lay
Upon the sacred altar the warm blood
Of slain affections, when they rise between
The soul and God.—

                    And can ye deem it strange
That from *their* planting such a branch should bloom
As nation's envy ?   Would a germ, embalmed
With prayer's pure tear-drops, strike no deeper root

Than that which mad ambition's hand doth strew
Upon the winds, to reap the winds again ?
Hid by its veil of waters from the hand
Of greedy Europe, their bold vine spread forth
In giant strength.—

                Its early clusters, crushed
In England's wine-press, gave the tyrant host
A draught of deadly wine.—O, ye who boast
In your free veins the blood of sires like these,
Lose not their lineaments.   Should Mammon cling
Too close around your heart,—or wealth beget
That bloated luxury which eats the core
From manly virtue,—or the tempting world
Make faint the Christian purpose in your soul,
Turn ye to Plymouth's beach,—and on that rock
Kneel in *their* footprints and renew the vow
They breathed to God.

                        Mrs. Sigourney.

THE PILGRIM FUNERAL.

It was a wintry scene,
  The hills were whiten'd o'er,
And the chill north winds were blowing keen
  Along the rocky shore.

Gone was the wood-bird's lay
  That the summer forest fills;
And the voice of the stream had pass'd away
  From its path among the hills;

And the low sun coldly smiled
  Through the boughs of the ancient wood,
Where a hundred souls—son, sire, wife, and child—
  Around a coffin stood.

They raised it gently up,
  And, through the untrodden snow,
They bore it away, with a solemn step,
  To a woody vale below;

And grief was in each eye
  As they moved towards the spot;
And brief low speech, and tear and sigh,
  Told that a friend was not.

When they laid his cold corpse low
    In its dark and narrow cell,
Heavy the mingled earth and snow
    Upon his coffin fell.

Weeping, they passed away,
    And left him there alone,
With no mark to tell where their dead friend lay,
    But the mossy forest stone.

When the winter storms were gone,
    And the strange birds sang around,
Green grass and violets sprung upon
    That spot of holy ground.

And o'er him giant trees
    Their proud arms toss'd on high,
And rustled music in the breeze
    That wandered through the sky.

When these were overspread
    With the leaves that autumn gave,
They bow'd them in the wind, and shed
    Their leaves upon his grave.

These woods are perished now,
    And that humble grave forgot,
And the yeoman sings as he draws his plough
    O'er that once sacred spot.

Two centuries are flown
　　Since they laid his cold corpse low,
And his bones are mouldered to dust, and strewn
　　To the breezes long ago.

And they who laid him there—
　　That sad and suffering train—
Now sleep in dust, to tell us where
　　No lettered stones remain,

Their memory remains ;
　　And ever shall remain,
More lasting than the aged fanes
　　Of Egypt's storied plain.

JOHN H. BRYANT.

BURIAL HILL AT PLYMOUTH.*

THE Pilgrim Fathers—where are they?
    The waves that brought them o'er
Still roll in the bay, and throw their spray,
    As they break along the shore;—
Still roll in the bay as they rolled that day
    When the Mayflower moored below,
When the sea around was black with storms,
    And white the shore with snow.

The mists that wrapped the pilgrims' sleep
    Still brood upon the tide;
And his rocks yet keep their watch by the deep,
    To stay its waves of pride:
But the snow-white sail, that he gave to the gale
    When the heavens looked dark, is gone:—
As an angel's wing, through an opening cloud,
    Is seen, and then withdrawn.

* COLE'S HILL, where the Pilgrims who died in the first winter were buried.
Their graves were smoothed, lest the Indians should learn the great extent of
mortality which prevailed. No traces now remain of these graves.

The pilgrim exile—sainted name !
    The hill, whose icy brow
Rejoiced, when he came, in the morning's flame—
    In the morning's flame burns now.
And the moon's cold light as it lay that night
    On the hill-side and the sea,
Still lies where he laid his houseless head :
    But the pilgrim—where is he ?

The Pilgrim Fathers are at rest ;
    When summer's throned on high,
And the world's warm breast is in verdure dressed,
    Go, stand on the hill where they lie.
The earliest ray of the golden day
    On that hallowed spot is cast ;
And the evening sun, as he leaves the world,
    Looks kindly on that spot last.

The pilgrim *spirit* has not fled,
    It walks in noon's broad light ;
And it watches the bed of the glorious dead,
    With the holy stars, by night.
It watches the bed of the brave who have bled,
    And shall guard this ice-bound shore
Till the waves of the bay, where the Mayflower lay,
    Shall foam and freeze no more.

                   REV. J. PIERPOINT.

Priscilla.

PRISCILLA, THE PILGRIM MAIDEN.*

Through the Plymouth woods John Alden went on his
    errand;
Came to an open space, and saw the disk of the ocean,
Sailless, sombre, and cold with the comfortless breath of
    the east-wind;
Saw the new-built house, and people at work in a
    meadow;
Heard, as he drew near the door, the musical voice of
    Priscilla
Singing the hundredth Psalm, the grand old Puritan
    anthem,
Music that Luther sang to the sacred words of the
    Psalmist,
Full of the breath of the Lord, consoling and comforting
    many.
Then, as he opened the door, he beheld the form of the
    maiden
Seated beside her wheel, and the carded wool like a
    snow-drift
Piled at her knee, her white hands feeding the ravenous
    spindle,
While with her foot on the treadle she guided the wheel
    in its motion.

* Priscilla Mullins, afterwards the wife of John Alden, above alluded to.

Open wide on her lap lay the well-worn psalm-book of
    Ainsworth,
Printed in Amsterdam, the words and the music
    together,
Rough-hewn, angular notes, like stones in the wall of a
    churchyard,
Darkened and overhung by the running vine of the
    verses.
Such was the book from whose pages she sang the old
    Puritan anthem,
She, the Puritan girl,* in the solitude of the forest,
Making the humble house and the modest apparel of
    home-spun
Beautiful with her beauty, and rich with the wealth of
    her being!

H. W. LONGFELLOW.

---

* The compiler respectfully takes exception to the term "Puritan" as
applied to the Pilgrim Fathers, or any one of their company. They were *Separatists*, but not *Puritans;* the distinctions between these parties are too important to admit of any tampering with the facts on this point. The Puritans
justified the intrusion of the powers of the State into the realms of conscience,
and invoked those powers to enforce their views. The Separatists—to their
eternal honour be it spoken—never persecuted, even in a persecuting age, and,
when called upon to do so, protested and voted against it, as utterly opposed to
Christ's teaching.   They were also the first in modern times to assert the abso-
lute supremacy of Christ in all matters concerning a Christian's conscience, and
the independence of Christ's Kingdom of the powers of the world.

THE MAYFLOWER RIDING AT ANCHOR.

EVENING.

Slowly as out of the heavens, with apocalyptical splen-
dors,
Sank the City of God, in the vision of John the Apostle,
So, with its cloudy walls of chrysolite, jasper, and
sapphire,
Sank the broad red sun, and over its turrets uplifted
Glimmered the golden reed of the angel who measured
the city.
Dimly the shadowy form of the Mayflower riding at
anchor,
Rocked on the rising tide, and ready to sail on the
morrow.————

MORNING.

————The village of Plymouth
Woke from its sleep, and arose, intent on its manifold
labors.
Sweet was the air and soft; and slowly the smoke from
the chimneys
Rose over roofs of thatch, and pointed steadily east-
ward;
Men came forth from the doors, and paused and talked
of the weather,

Said that the wind had changed, and was blowing fair
  for the Mayflower.
Merrily sang the birds, and the tender voices of women
Consecrated with hymns the common cares of the house-
  hold.
Out of the sea rose the sun, and the billows rejoiced at
  his coming;
Beautiful were his feet on the purple tops of the moun-
  tains;
Beautiful on the sails of the Mayflower riding at
  anchor,
Battered and blackened and worn by all the storms of
  the winter.
Loosely against her masts was hanging and flapping her
  canvas,
Rent by so many gales, and patched by the hands of the
  sailors.
Suddenly from her side, as the sun rose over the ocean,
Darted a puff of smoke, and floated seaward; anon rang
Loud over field and forest the cannon's roar, and the
  echoes
Heard and repeated the sound, the signal-gun of depar-
  ture!
Ah! but with louder echoes replied the hearts of the
  people!
Meekly, in voices subdued, the chapter was read from
  the Bible,
Meekly the prayer was begun, but ended in fervent
  entreaty!

Then from their houses in haste came forth the Pilgrims
  of Plymouth,
Men and women and children, all hurrying down to the
  sea-shore,
Eager, with tearful eyes, to say farewell to the Mayflower,
Homeward bound o'er the sea, and leaving them here in
  the desert. ———

H. W. Longfellow.

THE RETURN OF THE MAYFLOWER.

After remaining one hundred and ten days in Plymouth harbour, this historical
   and gallant little ship returned to England in April, 1621; and, notwithstanding their reduction by death, their sufferings, perils, and privations, all the surviving Pilgrims remained at their posts; *not one
   re-embarked.*

O STRONG hearts and true! not one went back in the
   Mayflower!
No, not one looked back, who had set his hand to this
   ploughing!
Soon were heard on board the shouts and songs of the
   sailors
Heaving the windlass round, and hoisting the ponderous
   anchor.
Then the yards were braced, and all sails set to the
   west-wind,
Blowing steady and strong; and the Mayflower sailed
   from the harbour,
Rounded the point of the Gurnet, and leaving far to the
   southward
Island and cape of sand, and the " Field of the First
   Encounter,"*

* So called from the encounter with the Indians on the first landing of the
Pilgrims.

Took the wind on her quarter, and stood for the open
  Atlantic,
Borne on the send of the sea, and the swelling hearts
  of the Pilgrims.
Long in silence they watched the receding sail of the
  vessel,
Much endeared to them all, as something living and
  human;
Then, as if filled with the spirit, and wrapt in a vision
  prophetic,
Baring his hoary head, the excellent Elder of Plymouth,
Said, " Let us pray!" and they prayed, and thanked the
  Lord and took courage.
Mournfully sobbed the waves at the base of the rock,
  and above them
Bowed and whispered the wheat on the "Hill of Death,"*
  and their kindred
Seemed to awake in their graves, and to join in the
  prayer that they uttered!
Sun-illumined and white, on the eastern verge of the
  ocean
Gleamed the departing sail, like a marble slab in a
  graveyard;
Buried beneath it lay, for ever, all hope of escaping.

H. W. LONGFELLOW.

* COLE'S HILL, where the Pilgrims who died in the first winter were buried.
Their graves were smoothed lest the Indians should observe them and learn the
extent of the mortality which had taken place. No traces now remain of these
graves.

ROBINSON OF LEYDEN.

HE sleeps not here; in hope and prayer
 His wandering flock had gone before;
But he, the shepherd, might not share
 Their sorrows on the wintry shore.

Before the Speedwell's anchor swung,
 Ere yet the Mayflower's sail was spread,
While round his feet the Pilgrims clung,
 The pastor spake, and thus he said:—

"Men, brethren, sisters, children dear!
 God calls you hence from over sea;
Ye may not build by Haarlem Meer,
 Nor yet along the Zuyder-Zee.

"Yet go to bear the saving word
 To tribes unnamed and shores untrod;
Heed well the lessons ye have heard
 From those old teachers taught of God.

"Yet think not unto them was lent
 All light for all the coming days,
And Heaven's eternal wisdom spent
 In making straight the ancient ways.

"The living fountain overflows
 For every flock, for every lamb;
Nor heeds, though angry creeds oppose
 With Luther's dike or Calvin's dam."

He spake : with lingering, long embrace,
    With tears of love and partings fond,
They floated down the creeping Maas,
    Along the isle of Ysselmond.

They passed the frowning towers of Briel,
    The " Hook of Holland's" shelf of sand,
And grated soon with lifting keel
    The sullen shores of Fatherland.

No home for these !—too well they knew
    The mitred king behind his throne ;
The sails were set, the pennons flew,
    And westward ho ! for worlds unknown.

—And these were they who gave us birth,
    The Pilgrims of the sunset wave,
Who won for us this virgin earth ;
    And freedom with the soil they gave.

The pastor slumbers by the Rhine,—
    In alien earth the exiles lie,—
Their nameless graves our holiest shrine,
    His words our noblest battle-cry !

Still cry them, and the world shall hear,
    Ye dwellers by the storm-swept sea !
Ye *have* not built by Haarlem Meer,
    Nor on the land-locked Zuyder-Zee.

                        OLIVER WENDELL HOLMES.

ELDER BREWSTER'S CHAIR.*

When this old chair was new,
    The manners of the times,
I now will bring to view;
    Take heed unto my rhymes.
Two hundred years and more,
    If history be true,
Since our forefathers came ashore,
    When this old chair was new.

They reared an humble roof,
    All pleasant to the sight;
Their ship was far aloof,
    It caught on fire at night.
Cold lodgings on the ground
    Oft made their hearts to rue;
While deadly arrows flew around,
    When this old chair was new.

No neighbourhood was theirs,
    Save natives of the land;
And many wants and cares,
    And winter was at hand.

* The Chair of Elder Brewster, first pastor of the Pilgrims, is still preserved in the Museum at Plymouth.

Good neighbourhood's sincerity
 They never failed to shew;
Their daily word was verity
 When this old chair was new.

Their bread on waters cast
 In future blessings found,
While hardships knit them fast
 Still bade them yet abound.
Full humble were their meals,
 Their dainties very few;
'Twas only ground nuts, clams, or eels,
 When this old chair was new.

Their greeting very soft,
 Good-morrow very kind,
How sweet it sounded oft,
 Before we were refined.
Humility their care,
 Their failings very few;
My heart! how kind their manners were,
 When this old chair was new.

THE MAIDEN PILGRIM'S PRAYER.

It may not be considered inappropriate to rescue from comparative oblivion a sweet prayer of one of the Maiden Pilgrims, by including it in these "*Lays.*" It is found worked upon the sampler of Lora, daughter of the celebrated Captain Miles Standish, which is still preserved amongst the relics of the Pilgrims at the New Plymouth Museum.

Lora Standish is my name.

Lord, guide my heart that I may do Thy will,
And fill my hands with such convenient skill,
As may conduce to virtue void of shame,
And I will give the glory to Thy name.

Pilgrim Relics.

STORY OF THE PILGRIMS.

Written in the year 1820.

COME, listen to my story,
  Though often told before,
Of men who pass'd to glory
  Through toil and travail sore ;
Of men who did for conscience sake
  Their native land forego,
And sought a home and freedom here
  Two hundred years ago.*

O, 'twas no earthborn passion
  That bade the adventurers stray ;
The world and all its fashion
  With them had passed away.
A voice from heaven bade them look
  Above the things below,
When here they sought a resting place,
  Two hundred years ago.

O, dark the scene and dreary,
  When here they set them down ;
Of storms and billows weary,
  And chilled with winter's frown.
Deep moan'd the forest to the wind,
  Loud howl'd the savage foe,
While here their evening prayer arose,
  Two hundred years ago.

* A.D. 1620.

'Twould drown the heart in sorrow
    To tell of all their woes;
No respite could they borrow,
    But from the grave's repose.
Yet nought could daunt the Pilgrim band,
    Or sink their courage low,
Who came to plant the Gospel here ·
    Two hundred years ago.

With humble prayer and fasting,
    In every strait and grief,
They sought the Everlasting,
    And found a sure relief.
Their Cov'nant God o'ershadow'd them,
    Their shield from every foe,
And gave them here a dwelling-place
    Two hundred years ago.

Of fair New England's glory
    They laid the corner stone;
This praise, in deathless story,
    Their grateful sons shall own.
Prophetic, they foresaw in time,
    A mighty state should grow,
From them, a few, faint Pilgrims here,
    Two hundred years ago.

If greatness be in daring,
    Our Pilgrim sires were great,
Whose sojourn here, unsparing
    Disease and famine wait;

And oft their treach'rous foes combine
    To lay the stranger low,
While founding here their commonwealth
    Two hundred years ago.

Though seeming over zealous
    In things by us deem'd light,
They were but duly jealous
    Of Power usurping Right.
They nobly chose to part with all
    Most dear to men below,
To worship here their God in peace
    Two hundred years ago.

From seeds they sowed with weeping,
    Our richest harvests rise ;
We still the fruits are reaping
    Of Pilgrim enterprise.
Then grateful we to them will pay
    The debt of fame we owe,
Who planted here the tree of life
    Two hundred years ago.

As comes this period yearly,
    Around our cheerful fires,
We'll think and tell how dearly
    Our comforts cost our sires.
For them we 'll wake the votive song,
    And bid the canvas glow,
Who fix'd the home of freedom here
    Two hundred years ago.
                 REV. DR. FLINT.

PILGRIM INFLUENCE.

WE owe allegiance to the State; but deeper, truer, more,
To the sympathies that God hath set within our spirits'
  core;—
Our country claims our fealty; we grant it so, but then
Before man made us citizens, great Nature made us
  men.

He's true to God who's true to man; wherever wrong
  is done,
To the humblest and the weakest, 'neath the all-behold-
  ing sun,
That wrong is also done to us; and they are slaves
  most base,
Whose love of right is for themselves, and not for all
  their race.

God works for all. Ye cannot bear the hope of being
  free
With parallels of latitude, with mountain-range or sea.
Put golden padlocks on Truth's lips, be callous as ye
  will,
From soul to soul o'er all the world, leaps one electric
  thrill.

Chain down your slaves with ignorance; ye cannot
  keep apart,
With all your craft of tyranny, the human heart from
  heart.
When first the Pilgrims landed on the Bay State's iron
  shore,
The Word went forth that slavery should one day be no
  more.*

JAMES RUSSELL LOWELL.

---

* It is a striking fact that the first cargo of African slaves was landed from an English ship at the Virginian Settlement in the year 1620—the very year in which the Pilgrim Fathers landed in Plymouth Bay, New England; so that slavery, as a system, and pilgrim principles were simultaneously planted in American soil, to carry on henceforth an irreconcilable conflict, until one or other of them shall be master of the field. It may temper the first feelings of shame which we, as Englishmen, experience when we reflect that we innoculated our American colonies with the virus of slavery, thrusting it upon some against their just protest, to reflect also that it was Englishmen (though proscribed and expatriated) who introduced into America the principles which must finally destroy slavery there and elsewhere. The operation of those principles have extirpated it in the Northern States, have prevented its blight from resting on the West, and will ultimately compass its destruction in the Southern States, of which the triumph of LINCOLN and HAMLIN, by the suffrages of the whole Union, may be accepted as the omen.

It may be interesting to mention that the first Stone of the Memorial Building in Southwark was laid by CYRUS HAMLIN, D.D., first cousin to HAMLIN, the Vice-President Elect of the United States.

WE ARE ONE.

THOUGH ages long have past
    Since our fathers left their home,
Their pilot in the blast,
    O'er untravelled seas to roam—
Yet lives the blood of England in our veins :
        And shall we not proclaim
        That blood of honest fame,
        Which no tyranny can tame
                By its chains ?

While the language free and bold,
    Which the bard of Avon sung,
In which our Milton told
    How the vault of heaven rung
When Satan, blasted, fell with all his host ;
        While these, with reverence meet,
        Ten thousand echoes greet,
        And from rock to rock repeat,
                Round our coast ;

While the manners, while the arts,
    That mould a nation's soul,
Still cling around our hearts,
    Between, let ocean roll,
Our joint communion breaking with the sun ;
        Yet still, from either beach,
        The voice of blood shall reach
        More audible than speech,
              We are one.

                WASHINGTON ALLSTON.

THE SONG OF THE DUMB.

H. R. H. the Prince of Wales, on the occasion of his recent visit to the DEAF AND DUMB INSTITUTION of New York, was greeted with the following welcome, written by Mrs. Peet, and recited in the sign-language by Miss Gertrude Walter.

WELCOME TO THE PRINCE.

ONCE from beyond the azure sea
    There came to us a welcome tone.
Men paused amid their strife and toil,
    To list the voice from England's throne.

And soon from out the ocean's depths,
    Where master minds a CHAIN* had bound,
A strong pulsation shook the land,
    And silence hushed the New World's sound.

How breathlessly men stopped to count
    The throbs that came with measured beat,
Till one by one, with trembling joy,
    Beheld the mystic bond complete.

* The Atlantic telegraphic cable.

The strange, new thrill sped fast and far,
    And waking joy throughout the land,
Went forth the greeting England sent,
    "We'll ever more go hand in hand."*

Old Ocean, in his wild dismay,
    That man from him his power had won
To part the nations, rent the bond;
    But England sends us now her son.

Right loyally we greet him, too,
    For every heart should bend, I ween,
In homage to such worth as that
    Which sits enthroned in England's Queen.

And though no purples hang above
    The brave and youthful Briton here,
Yet retinues of kindred hearts
    Send up to heaven their loyal cheer:

"God save the Queen—God save the Prince,
    And blessings on them richly shower,
And strengthen every righteous cause
    That adds to England's rightful power."

                                    MRS. PEET.

---

* The Telegraphic Message:—"FROM H. M. THE QUEEN OF GREAT BRITAIN TO HIS EXCELLENCY THE PRESIDENT OF THE UNITED STATES.—The Queen desires to congratulate the President upon the successful completion of this great international work, in which the Queen has taken the greatest interest. The Queen is convinced that the President will join with her in fervently hoping that the electric cable, which now already connects Great Britain with the United States, will prove an *additional link between the two nations, whose friendship is founded upon their common interest and reciprocal esteem.* The Queen has much pleasure in thus directly communicating with the President, and in renewing to him her best wishes for the prosperity of the United States."

OUR FATHERS' LAND.

INTERNATIONAL ODE.*

GOD bless our Fathers' Land,
Keep her in heart and hand
   One with our own !
From all her foes defend,
Be her brave people's friend,
On all her realms descend ;
   Protect her throne !

Father, in loving care,
Guard Thou her kingdom's heir,
   Guide all his ways :
Thine arm his shelter be
From harm by land and sea ;
Bid storm and danger flee ;
   Prolong his days !

Lord, let war's tempest cease,
Fold the whole earth in peace
   Under Thy wings !
Make all Thy nations one,
All hearts beneath the sun,
Till Thou shalt reign alone,
   Great King of kings !

O. W. HOLMES.

* Sung by a vast assembly of Scholars in the Music Hall, Boston, Mass., on the occasion of the visit of H. R. H. the Prince of Wales.

PILGRIM LAMPS.

THESE Mayflower lights, whose quickening rosy gleams,
   So faint, at first, but growing like the morn,
Wide round the world now send their kindling beams
   Of truth and freedom, ushering in the dawn.

Children of faith,—they walked by future light;
   The glory not yet come illumed their way:
In truth's great conflict, champions for the right,—
   Tender, yet stern, they wrestled out their way.

Free worship and free thought they claimed, and found;
   Our larger golden freedom gathers rust—
Too oft our banner stoops to kiss the ground;
   We have more sunlight, but 'tis flecked with dust.

Away with liberty that leaves man free,
   Unlicensed on his fellow-man to prey!
When law, truth, virtue are trod down by thee,
   O, faithless freedom, we disown thy sway.

Ye sons, think deep; be strong in heart and hand;
   Remember God, who, with His silver key,
Unlocked the western gates, and gave this land
   To freedom's sons, and all whom truth makes free.

Fast rush the future ages into light,—
  Come, halcyon peace, on that broad ocean sail!
Long may the lamps in Pilgrim tombs burn bright:
  FOR EVER PILGRIM PRINCIPLES PREVAIL.

F. W. CAULKINS.

The End.

London: Thomas Harrild, Printer, Shoe Lane, Fleet Street.

BY THE SAME AUTHOR.

AN HOUR WITH THE PILGRIM FATHERS AND THEIR PRECURSORS:

A Lecture.

LONDON: LONGMANS & Co.   Price 8*d*.

"This is a genuine *multum in parvo* history of a period, from which dates many great events in English and American annals.   It was compiled at the suggestion of friends of religious freedom, from the work of Mr. W. H. Bartlett, and from documents recently discovered by Mr. Waddington amongst the "Lambeth," "Harleian," "Lansdowne," and "State Paper Office" MSS., and from the deeply interesting MS. volume in the handwriting of Governor Bradford, also recently found in the Bishop's Library at Fulham."—*City Press.*

DIAGRAMS

Illustrative of the above Lecture.

A Set of Ten, price 30s., comprising the following subjects :—

BARROW AND GREENWOOD IN PRISON. . CICELY WAITING FOR COPY.
MARTYRDOM OF PENRY AT ST. THOMAS-A-WATERING.
MAP—NORTH-EAST PART OF ENGLAND.
SITE OF MANOR HOUSE AT SCROOBY.
AUSTERFIELD CHURCH, STANDISH CHAPEL, ETC.
DELFTHAVEN, SCENE ON THE MAESE.
THE "MAYFLOWER" AND "SPEEDWELL" IN DARTMOUTH HARBOUR.
CAPE COD HARBOUR, WITH THE "MAYFLOWER."
PLAN OF NEW PLYMOUTH BAY, NEW ENGLAND.
RELICS OF THE PILGRIMS IN THE PLYMOUTH MUSEUM.

WORKING MEN'S EDUCATIONAL UNION,

25, KING WILLIAM STREET, STRAND, W.C.

BY THE SAME AUTHOR.

Second Edition.   Fourth Thousand.

THE CONTENTS AND TEACHINGS OF THE
CATACOMBS AT ROME.

A Vindication of Pure and Primitive Christianity, and an Exposure of the
Corruptions of Popery, Derived from the Sepulchral Remains
of the Early Christians at Rome.

LONDON: LONGMANS & Co.

Octavo, price 2s. 6d. cloth.

"We are gratified but not surprised that this admirable volume has reached
a Second Edition. The Lecturer points out with most convincing clearness the
sure foundation on which the Christian religion is built up, and produces from
the sculptured stones of the Catacombs many a valuable sermon of Christian
doctrine. The Author's object is gained if his volume is well received by the
operative class, for whom the Lectures were originally designed; but their popular form, we are persuaded, will recommend them not less to the great mass of
the reading public, especially to those who have not read, or may not have it in
their power to possess themselves of the larger work by Dr. Maitland."—*Scot-
tish Guardian.*

"This book was originally designed for working men; but we apprehend
that many besides working men will be glad to avail themselves of its assistance.
The book is, however, not only a course of lectures on the Catacombs; it gives
also a popular account of Paganism, of Popery, and of Christianity, and it uses
the Catacombs chiefly as furnishing a vindication of pure and primitive Christianity, and an exposure of the corruptions of Popery. In the form of lectures
it was both interesting and useful: in its present form it will be both, much
more extensively."—*Freeman.*

"We strongly recommend our young friends in general to possess themselves
of a copy of Mr. Scott's valuable and interesting Lectures."—*Patriot.*

"No testimony, except that of Scripture, can be more authentic. Mr. Scott
has done good service in publishing the evidence of such a witness to the truth
of our reformed Christianity."—*The Bulwark.*

"The substance of our knowledge regarding the Catacombs at Rome is com-
pressed into this little volume. Rome concealed in its most corrupt period the
evidences of its errors, to be excavated in our times, like the monuments of
Egypt and the ruins of Nineveh, as witnesses to the truth. The work contains
passages of great interest."—*Expositor.*

Diagrams to illustrate the above Lectures can be obtained of Mr. F. Baker,
25, King William Street, Strand, W.C.

Lists sent on receipt of a Postage Stamp.

BY THE SAME AUTHOR.

Third Thousand,

THE REVIVAL IN ULSTER; ITS SOCIAL AND MORAL RESULTS.

LONDON: LONGMANS & Co.

Price 1s.; by post, free, 1s. 2d.

" Mr. Scott's pamphlet is a repertory of authenticated facts."—*The Eclectic Review.*

"If any one desires more facts, let him read the pamphlet of Mr. Scott."—*London Review.*

"For any future history of the revival in Ulster, Mr. Scott's compilation will be valuable material. It is evidence, not in the mouth of two or three witnesses, but of sixty—not of clergyman only, but of laymen—not of one body of Christians, but, with a single exception, of all—not of Irishmen only, but of Scotch and English—not of private persons only, but of Bishops, Archdeacons, Professors, Members of Parliament, a Roman Catholic Judge, an Earl, a Countess, and the Lord Lieutenant."—*Watchman.*

" Its arguments and tone command attention; it wears no trace of excitement, no colour of enthusiasm in its composition; it is written with judicial severity and plainness; it collates the testimony of unprejudiced witnesses, of every rank and profession, as to the simple facts they had seen ; and records the author's own observations with naked accuracy ;—and so doing it bears home upon the mind of the reader the conviction, that the revival of religion in Ulster is a work of God, with a conclusive force which no honest and candid mind can resist."—*Patriot.*

" The pamphlet of Mr. Scott contains a calm review of the rise, progress, and present position of this most marvellous movement. The evidence which he adduces in support of the proposition, that the revival is the work of the Divine Spirit, is so ample and conclusive that no intelligent and unbiassed mind could possibly oppose a successful resistance."—*Morning Advertiser.*

" The book will, we doubt not, soon be in the hands of thousands. Let it be read in families, in class meetings, in prayer meetings, in social meetings."—*Wesleyan Times.*

" Mr. Scott's book is one of considerable value, and we recommend all those who are still sceptical as to read it, and they will be convinced that the movement is a genuine one, and that God alone can be its Author."—*City Press.*

" It is a pamphlet which ought to be in the library of every Christian, as a conscientious and truthful record of the varied experiences of some hundred ministers and laymen in connection with the spiritual awakening of 1859."—*Banner of Ulster.*

" We have seen nothing on the revival at all to be compared with this pamphlet —a pamphlet crammed with facts as well as opinions. The author says truly that if the testimony of more than sixty credible witnesses does not convince, nothing will. Mr. Scott has done good service to the Church of Christ by the publication of this pamphlet. His own opinion of the revival is exceedingly important, and here it is backed up with testimony which cannot be rejected or doubted. We advise our readers to order the pamphlet as the most satisfactory on the subject."—*Glasgow Examiner.*

" Well adapted to remove the doubts and objections of those who have looked unfavourable on the movement."—*Glasgow Commonwealth.*

" A most valuable compilation, throwing full light upon the social and moral results."—*National Standard.*

BY THE SAME AUTHOR.

Fourth Edition.

PRACTICAL HINTS

TO

UNPRACTISED LECTURERS TO THE WORKING CLASSES.

With a Catalogue of Diagrams, etc., published to aid Lecturers; and Lists of
Subjects Lectured upon by Correspondents of the
Working Men's Educational Union.

LONDON: F. BARON, King William Street, W.C.

Price 8d.

BY THE SAME AUTHOR.

Second Thousand.

THE SABBATH WREATH.

A Selection of Sacred Poetry on the Anticipation and Retrospect, Ordinances,
Employments, Privileges, and Enjoyments of the Lord's Day.

LONDON: WERTHEIM AND MACINTOSH, Paternoster Row.

149 pp., cloth, gilt edges,

Price 1s. 6d.

THE PROGRESS OF LOCOMOTION.

Being Two Lectures on the Advances made in Artificial Locomotion in
Great Britain.

LONDON: F. BARON, King William Street, W.C.

Price 1s.

These Lectures are illustrated by Diagrams, to be obtained of Mr. F.
Baron, as above.

LONGFELLOW'S POEM ON THE PILGRIM FATHERS.

In fcap. 4to, price 7s. 6d., cloth, elegantly gilt,

THE

COURTSHIP OF MILES STANDISH,

AND OTHER POEMS.

By HENRY WADSWORTH LONGFELLOW.

Beautifully illustrated by JOHN GILBERT, and splendidly printed on toned paper by Mr. CLAY.

"A VERITABLE WORK OF ART."—*The Times.*

In fcap. 4to, price 21s., cloth, gilt edges, or in morocco elegant, 31s. 6d.,

BUNYAN'S PILGRIM'S PROGRESS.

Edited by GEORGE OFFOR,

And Illustrated with 110 Original Designs by J. G. WATSON.

Engraved in the first style by DALZIELS,

And printed by Mr. CLAY, on the finest toned paper.

The Times, Dec. 24th, 1860.

"We can praise this work without stint for drawing, composition, treatment, and characterization of the highest class, and we do so none the less cordially that the artist's name was unknown, until by this veritable *chef-d'œuvre* he has made his mark with a bound.

"When this book has tumbled out of its heavy boards it will be worthily preserved, as an example of the better art amongst us, while other men were scratching, stippling, fumbling, and smearing pages with gold and vermilion. Taken altogether, the entire volume is one of the most beautiful and satisfactory that we have seen for years."

The Manchester News and Express.

"A more beautiful book, in every respect, we have not yet seen. It is as good as it is handsome, and as cheap as it is excellent."

Oriental Budget.

"In illustrated books *Routledge's Pilgrim's Progress* is by far the best, and it is remarkable as bringing out the capacities of a new illustrator, Mr. Watson, of Manchester."

The Examiner.

"Great praise is due to the artist for the pictures in this beautiful edition of Bunyan. All the figures are well drawn, and what ninety-nine persons out of a hundred would see in the mind's eye as they read, is here presented in a sound artistic manner. To the taste of a large and worthy section of the public we highly commend it."

Daily News.

"To sum up the merits of this work, we certainly pronounce it to be the completest and handsomest edition of 'The Pilgrim's Progress' that has ever come under our observation."

ROUTLEDGE, WARNE, & ROUTLEDGE,

FARRINGDON STREET, LONDON.

In the Press,

NEW WORK BY DOCTOR WADDINGTON.

———

THE TRACK OF THE HIDDEN CHURCH;

OR,

THE SPRINGS OF THE PILGRIM MOVEMENT.

1559—1620.

BY JOHN WADDINGTON, D.D.

WITH AN INTRODUCTION

BY EDWARD N. KIRK, D.D.

———

LONDON: LONGMANS & Co., Paternoster Row.